THE TREASURE AT NORTH BERWICK

Published in Great Britain by
SERAFINA PRESS
The Smokehouse Gallery
St Ellas Place
Eyemouth
Berwickshire
TD14 5HP

www.serafinapress.co.uk

ISBN 0-9552696-7-9
ISBN 978-0-9552696-7-7

First published in Great Britain in 2010

Printed in Great Britain by Martins the Printers
Berwick upon Tweed
www.martins-the-printers.com

For my IFS Edinburgh 2010
colleagues - beloved, all.
Also for Kathy Zuckerman, across the miles.
And for Carole Boyle, closer to home.

J.T.D.

The Treasure at North Berwick

BY JENNIFER T. DOHERTY ILLUSTRATED BY SOPHIE ELM

SERAFINA
PRESS

Every Summer, Peter went to stay with his Granny May in the seaside town of North Berwick. And every Summer, he liked to meet his friend Bonnie, who also came on holiday to the town.

On his first night there, he ran down to the BEACH to
LOOK for BONNIE. Granny May's dogs, FLOSS
and ROSS, raced along beside him.

Bass Rock...

The TIDE was out, and plenty of CHILDREN were playing in the GOLDEN EVENING LIGHT, but there was NO SIGN of BONNIE. PETER looked around. "She must still be at HOME", he thought, a little DISAPPOINTED. Then he noticed a line of PEBBLES ...in the... SAND, leading to their favourite ROCKS. BONNIE'S head PEEKED out from HIGH in the ROCK.

"How do you like my **FORT**?" she called.
"I have a **PICNIC** here for us."

"It's **MY** fort too", said Peter.

"I **PLAYED** here last **SUMMER**, you know, and I've brought some **APPLES** from Granny May's garden."

"**Climb up then**", said BONNIE.

"I Wonder if anything **EXCITING** will happen this summer..." said Bonnie, when they were comfy in the **ROCK FORT**.

"**WONDER IF ...**" said Peter, **GAZING** out to **Sea**.

EVERY DAY, WHEN IT WAS **SUNNY**, THEY PLAYED ON THE *Beaches* and WANDERED THROUGH TOWN FOR **ICE-CREAM** AND *Cupcakes.*

THEY WENT TO THE **SEABIRD CENTRE** and looked out TO THE ISLANDS AND THE **GREAT** *Rock* through **TELESCOPES** AND *Cameras* and **BINOCULARS.**

THEY GAZED as the ROCK changed colour with the shifting LIGHT, and took turns at naming Seabirds which swept and floated round the bay. Above all, they loved to watch the SWOOPING, DIVING GANNETS near the shore.

When it rained, Granny May enjoyed having Peter and Bonnie over to her flat. Sometimes, she liked to play with them, but other times she wanted to read her newspaper.

Then, she would tell them to run along and make up a **PLAY**, or to build a **BOAT** out of all the interesting *SHEETS* and *BOXES* and *UPSIDE-DOWN* furniture that they could find. But one damp morning, she set them a different task.

"Did you know that there's **TREASURE** at **NORTH BERWICK**?" she asked them. They shook their heads.

"There most certainly is. It's there for anyone to find, if they know how to look."

"Why hasn't anyone found it then?" asked Peter.

"**MAYBE THEY HAVE.**"

"Then why is it there if people have found it already?"

"Well, that's part of the

PUZZLE!

Why don't you have a look for it this summer?"

"If it is real **TREASURE**, will we be *rich*?" asked Bonnie. "Do you have a treasure map?"

"Oh, it's **REAL** treasure, but I'll leave it to you to **JUDGE WHAT IT'S WORTH**," said Granny May.

"And no~no map. But there is a **R H Y M E** I've known since I was a little girl. It might give you a **CLUE**.

GRANNY MAY

THEY PADDED DOWN TO THE **RATHER DAMP** AND SALTY FORT— THE TIDE HAD JUST **GONE OUT.**

"A THINK ABOUT IT?" SAID BONNIE. "SEEMS MORE LIKE WE SHOULD ▸ **DIG for TREASURE.**"

"Yes ~ TREASURE could be buried but **WHERE?**"

"The **BEACH** might be a good place to start. It's below the **WAVES** at high tide ~ FISHES would swim there. So it's a bit like the RHYME. NOT SURE ABOUT **SNOW** and **WISHES** though... Maybe we will figure that out", said Bonnie.

"OK", said Peter. "Tomorrow we start **DIGGING.**"

THEY DUG ON BOTH OF THE BEACHES.

THEY DUG ON THE SHORELINE AND CLOSE TO THE DUNES.

THEY DUG IN THE DUNES. (NOT SO EASY.)

AND, ONE AFTERNOON, THEY DUG IN THE EARTH OF THE BIG HILL OUTSIDE THE TOWN.

THEY EVEN DUG IN GRANNY MAY'S BACK GARDEN. BUT NO TREASURE DID THEY FIND... "HAVE YOU FIGURED IT OUT YET?" GRANNY MAY WOULD ASK, AND THEY WOULD HAVE TO ADMIT THAT THEY HADN'T.

ON CLEAR
DAYS,
AS THEY DUG IN
VAIN FOR THE
TREASURE,
. . .
THEY COULD SEE
LITTLE BOATS
Racing
‣ ACROSS THE BAY. ◂

KITTEWAKES

PUFFINS

THEIR BOAT bobbed SLOWLY in the water, then **TOOK OFF.** OUT IT WHIZZED, round the islands. They all looked for PUFFINS and KITTEWAKES **AND SEALS.**

seal

Then the guide said,

"HOLD ON!"

~ and they
BOUNCED OUT
towards →
THE GREAT...

BASS ROCK
IN THE BAY.

...Kur Kur...

...Kur Kur...

THE LIGHTHOUSE

As they got nearer to the Rock, the sky changed. Above them, round and round flew hundreds of huge white gannets. Bits of nest-straw floated through the air, along with old white down from the chicks, and larger scraps of feather. The gannets called and called. All the grown-ups were taking photos, but Peter and Bonnie were too excited. They nudged each other.

GANNETS

"The *feathers* ~ just like **SNOW**!" Said Bonnie. "**WHERE SNOW FLIES**! This is it ~ this is . . .

. . . **THE TREASURE AT** *North* **BERWICK!**" Shouted Peter. "It's all in the rhyme after all."

"**FISHES**, yes ~ the **GANNETS** eat those. And **WAVES** ~ of course." (The boat lurched a bit.) "And you can't help look up at the **SKY**. But what about the **WISHES**?" Said Bonnie.

Back ashore, they raced over to Granny May's. **"WE'VE SOLVED THE RIDDLE!"** they shouted, as they clattered upstairs. "At Least we THINK so… we saw the snowy GANNETS ~ they are the **treasure**, aren't they?

We know about the waves and the sky ~ but what about the WISHES?" Said Peter. GRANNY MAY S M I L E D.

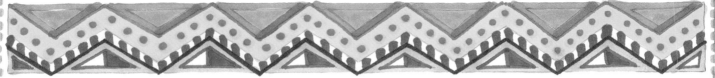

"Ah~that's easy. The story goes that you get a **WISH** ~all for yourself~ when the FIRST **GANNET** of the season LANDS ON THE **ROCK** in JANUARY OR **FEBRUARY.**

And you make a **WISH**~ for someone else~ when the LAST **GANNET** goes, round about **OCTOBER.**"

"Where do they go?" asked BONNIE.

"All the way down to **WEST** AFRICA. They stay there in the **SUNSHINE** till it's time to come BACK to **NORTH BERWICK.**"

"We won't be here when the first **GANNET** comes back," said PETER, disappointed.

"We won't even be here when the **LAST** one goes."

WEST AFRICA

"Don't you worry about that", said Granny May. "I'll make sure you find out when to make your wishes. Because you found it ~ the wonderful colony of GANNETS at BASS Rock IS the TREASURE. Now, I think we should celebrate, don't you?"

POSTCARD

Peter
36 Ced
ED
E H

GAN

Dear Peter,
As promised,
I send you news of
our first Gannet
arrivals. Don't forget
your wishes!

Much Love
Granny May ×××